Let's Eat BUGS!

Reycraft Books
145 Huguenot Street
New Rochelle, NY 10801

Reycraftbooks.com

Reycraft Books is a trade imprint and trademark of Newmark Learning, LLC.

Library of Congress Control Number: 2021902290

Hardcover ISBN: 978-1-4788-7403-4
Paperback ISBN: 978-1-4788-7402-7

Printed in Dongguan, China. 949559/0525/22735

10 9 8 7 6 5 4

First Edition published by Reycraft Books 2021

Reycraft Books and Newmark Learning, LLC, support diversity and the First Amendment, and celebrate the right to read.

Photo Credits: Front Cover, Jacket Front, Pages 6, 7A, 8, 9B, 10A, 12, 16, 20, 24, 25B, 27, 28, 32, 36, 37A, 40B, Inside Back Flap B: Ilán Rabchinskey Photography; Title Page, Pages 17C, 17E, 18B, 18C, 18D, 19A: NERYXCOM/Shutterstock; Page 4: RONALDO SCHEMIDT/Getty Images; Page 5A: Shelly MD Photography/Shutterstock; Page 5B: Oleksii Synelnykov/Shutterstock; Page 7B: Hemis/Alamy; Pages 9A, 25A: mr.kie/Shutterstock; Page 9C: Charoen Krung Photography/Shutterstock; Page 9D: Taweesak Sriwannawit/Shutterstock; Page 10B: Foodcollection/Getty Images; Page 10C: Brian Overcast/Alamy; Page 11: Marcelino Martinez Aguirre/Wikimedia Commons; Page 13A: Dmytro Khlystun/Shutterstock; Page 13B: Rachel Kolokoff Hopper/Alamy; Page 13C: EyeEm/Alamy; Page 14A: Athapet Piruksa/Shutterstock; Page 14B: nicemyphoto/Shutterstock; Page 14C: ElHielo/Shutterstock; Page 15: Alex Ramsay/Alamy; Page 17A: imageBROKER/Alamy; Page 17B: ineskoleva/Getty Images; Page 17D: Marcelo Rodriguez/Shutterstock; Page 18A: Keith Dannemiller/Alamy; Page 19B: NATALIA MAMYSHEVA/Alamy; Page 21A: bug eye Thailand/Getty Images; Page 21B: Lingbeek/Getty Images; Page 21C: rainmax/Getty Images; Page 22A: April Nobile/AntWeb.org; Pages 22B, 22C: THE WHITE CAT PHOTOGRAPHY/Shutterstock; Page 23: JesusTphotog/Shutterstock; Page 26A: Ernie Cooper/Shutterstock; Page 26B: Juan de Tovar/Courtesy John Carter Brown Library; Page 29A: DimaSid/Shutterstock; Page 29B: Gerry Bishop/Shutterstock; Page 30A: Lee waranyu/Shutterstock; Page 30B: Againstar/Shutterstock; Page 31A: Anna_Pustynnikova/Shutterstock; Page 31B: Gonzalo1978/Getty Images; Page 33A: The natures/Shutterstock; Page 33B: Achkin/Shutterstock; Page 34A: ilkah/Shutterstock; Page 34B: ANDA_Photos/Shutterstock; Page 35: seagames50 images/Shutterstock; Page 37B: Mark Christopher Cooper/Shutterstock; Page 37C: yod67/Shutterstock; Page 38A: Windy Soemara/Getty Images; Page 38B: sunakri/Shutterstock; Page 39A: Tatiana Volgutova/Shutterstock; Page 39B: Lewis Tse Pui Lung/Shutterstock; Page 40A, Inside Back Flap A: Provided by Judy Goldman; Back Cover, Jacket Back: sruilk/Shutterstock

Let's Eat BUGS!

by Judy Goldman
photography by Ilán Rabchinskey

Mexicans eat LOTS of insects.

And they don't do it because there's nothing else to eat. They do it because they want to. They do it because they're delicious!

Insects are the largest group of living beings. They can be found almost everywhere on the planet. They come in different sizes, and are of many colors and forms. Some have wings and lots of legs.

They creep. They buzz. They whirl and enchant.

Some can bite, and others can be scary. Several can be very organized.

Others can camouflage themselves so well that when they're on tree trunks, rocks, or leaves, they seem to become part of them!

They're an important part of the chain of life because they eat other bugs and many of them are food for bigger insects and animals such as reptiles, fish, amphibians, birds, and mammals. This helps keep their populations controlled. Why? Otherwise, there would be so many insects everywhere they could cause sickness, damage crops, and fill every corner of your house. You wouldn't be able to live there anymore!

During pre-Hispanic times, the basic foods of the native groups of Mexico were corn, chilies, squash, and beans. They also dined on duck, fish, collared peccary, deer, turkey, diverse fruits, and many other types of vegetables. Plus lots of insects. After the conquest, some Spaniards believed that eating bugs was a custom of savages. So they tried to prohibit, or stop, people from eating them. Fortunately, lots of people didn't pay attention and, thanks to the women who taught their daughters and granddaughters how to prepare them, many of the recipes survived.

Bugs can be tasty!

They are also good for you because they have minerals and proteins your body needs. Besides, depending on the species and time of the year, they're easy to find, dry, and prepare, and can be stored for a long time. That doesn't mean you should run out to the garden, park, or forest and eat the first bug you find. Most are not edible.

Now, let's get to know some tasty insects and the recipes for preparing them. Ask an adult to prepare them. Or try it on your own with an adult's help. Also, if you're allergic to bug bites, it's best not to eat them. You'll just have to take our word that they're very good.

Gusanos de maguey

This worm is the larva of a moth. It is more or less the length of your pinky. Once the eggs hatch, and before they become moths, the larvae bore holes into leaves of the maguey, a type of agave plant. There they make tunnels to the mezontete. That's the heart of the plant, where sometimes 40 to 60 worms can live at the same time. They also spend their nymph stage inside the agave. Once they finish growing, they will emerge as moths.

They must be extracted, or removed, when they're still larvae. People do this by using a strip from the leaf of the maguey from which all the thorns have been removed except the one at the tip. This strip is then bent to form a hook that is used to catch the worm by the head.

When?

These worms are gathered during the rainy season.

What color are they?

Some are red and others are white.

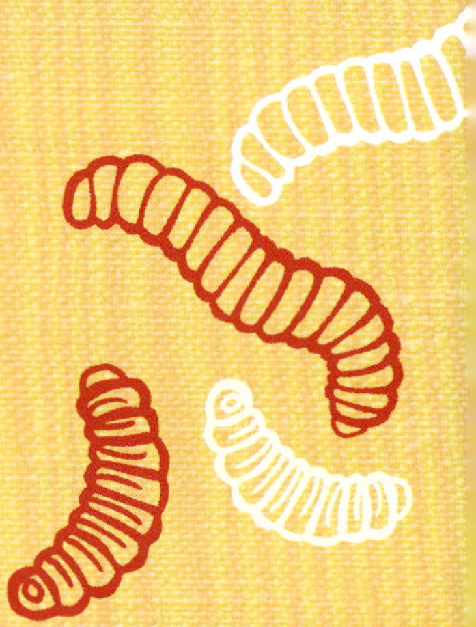

FUN FACT

They are so famous that they are eaten in faraway places like Japan.

- The eggs of the agave worm are covered in a film of natural glue. This helps them stay stuck on the agave leaf.
- When the worm is born, it breaks the film, bores a hole in the leaf, and enters about 12 centimeters into it.
- Due to its life cycle, three generations of worms—small, medium, and large—can be found inside the same plant.
- The red worms are found mainly in the states of Tlaxcala, Hidalgo, and Oaxaca. The white worms are from Tlaxcala, Hidalgo, and the State of Mexico.

- This worm is one of the most famous of Mexico's edible insects and is considered a delicacy. Nowadays, it is exported to Asia, Europe, and the United States.

Gusano de Maguey Appetizer

INGREDIENTS

- Gusanos de maguey
- Vegetable oil
- Salt, to taste
- Tortillas
- Guacamole
- Your favorite salsa

DIRECTIONS

Wash the worms well. Dry them. Then fry them (or toast them on a comal—a smooth, flat grill or griddle) until they blow up like little balloons and are browned and crunchy. Sprinkle them with salt. Warm a tortilla. Spread some guacamole on it—so the gusanos stick and don't spill out. Add a few worms, your favorite salsa, and enjoy!

Chapulines

When?

They are abundant during the rainy season.

What color are they?

Their color depends on the species and the places where they live. Usually they vary from green to brown.

Chapulines, or grasshoppers, are herbivores. That means they eat only plants, which they reach by using their long, strong legs to jump very high. The word chapulín comes from the Nahuatl language. It means "insect that bounces like a rubber ball."

In some places, like Oaxaca, lots of people go out to the fields to trap them. The smaller ones are found in alfalfa fields. The bigger ones are found in milpas (native cornfields.) Once they're gathered, they're put in a covered clay pot so that they can empty their digestive tracts. As soon as they're clean inside, they're washed, boiled, and toasted. Lime juice and salt are added, to taste.

FUN FACT

When the eggs hatch, the first grasshopper born makes a tunnel to the surface and the rest follow.

- There are thousands of varieties of grasshoppers around the world.
- When the Mexicas, who later became the Aztecs, arrived at a hill about 7 kilometers away from where they would later found their capital, Tenochtitlán, they found so many grasshoppers that they named that place Chapultepec. This name means "hill of the grasshopper." Chapultepec is the biggest park in Mexico City and one of the largest in the Western Hemisphere.

- The female, who produces between 400 and 500 eggs, generally lays them underground, sometimes near the roots of plants. Then she covers them in a foamy substance that will protect them.
- In many of the markets in Oaxaca, you will find people selling fried grasshoppers of different sizes—ranging from tiny to big. The small ones can be eaten whole and, for instance, sprinkled on guacamole. But sometimes it is best to remove the legs of the big ones so they don't get caught in your teeth.

Grasshoppers in Garlic

INGREDIENTS

- Toasted grasshoppers
- Chopped garlic, to taste
- Vegetable oil or butter
- Salt, to taste

DIRECTIONS

Heat the oil or butter in a pan. Add the garlic and sauté for a few minutes. Add the grasshoppers. Sauté for a few minutes more and add salt to taste.

Jumiles

When?

They are found under dry, fallen leaves after the rainy season.

What color are they?

They are dark brown.

A jumil is a type of stinkbug. It lives in oak trees. The females are larger than the males and have wings. So you have to take care that they don't fly away.

FUN FACT

The first Monday after the Day of the Dead, celebrated on the 1st and the 2nd of November, people gather on the Huixteco Mountain, near the silver-mining town of Taxco, Guerrero. There they celebrate the Day of the Sacred Jumil. Many of these people eat the insects because they believe they protect the population.

The best way to enjoy them is to eat them alive! When you put them into your mouth and chew, it will feel like fireworks have gone off inside your head. Why? They produce flavor explosions, similar to a strange mix of apple and anise seed. They will also make your mouth go to sleep.

- Because jumiles are sold live, many times they are put into a plastic basin with a cone inside. Both are greased so that the bugs can't crawl out.

- Jumiles secrete an analgesic and anesthetic substance, and this is why, when you eat them, your mouth will most probably fall asleep for a while.

- They produce an oily liquid that smells bad and keeps their predators away.

- They are eaten mainly in the states of Morelos and Guerrero but also in Veracruz, Hidalgo, and Oaxaca.

- You can eat them alive in a warm tortilla with salsa, but you need to make sure they don't escape out of the other side of the taco and wander around your face. Just use your finger to scrape them back and into your mouth and crunch away.

Jumiles in Guacamole

INGREDIENTS

- Chopped garlic
- Chopped onion
- Chopped serrano or jalapeño chilies
- Chopped fresh cilantro
- 100 grams of toasted jumiles
- 2 or 3 big avocados
- Salt, to taste

DIRECTIONS

Mix the onions, garlic, and chilies. Grind the jumiles with the cilantro. Peel the avocados and remove the seeds. Mash the avocado flesh. Add the other ingredients and mix until well blended. You can add some lime juice to prevent the guacamole from turning dark.

Escamoles

When?

They are gathered between April and May.

What color are they?

They are white.

Escamoles are the larvae of a type of red ant. They look like grains of rice. Farmers and people who live in the country look for the nests. When they find one, they gently remove the escamoles with their bare hands, even though they will be bitten many times. Why? When the ants feel that their nest is in danger, they carry the eggs and larvae away to hide them while others attack the intruder.

FUN FACT

Sometimes ant nests are invaded by other ants who take away the eggs. When those eggs hatch, those ants will be their slaves.

The escamoles need to be removed carefully so that no damage is done to the nests. These nests are usually found near or below maguey agave plants.

- When a female starts a new nest, she herself will feed the first larvae by regurgitating, or throwing up. Once they finish growing, these first workers will do everything so that the queen can spend all her time laying eggs.

- An ant larva is so tiny that it weighs approximately 0.0384 grams.

- Ant nests are subterranean and do not have clearly defined areas—unlike a beehive. Ants frequently move eggs and larvae from one section to another to maintain them at adequate temperature and humidity.

- If a nest remains in good condition, it can produce escamoles for 40 years.

Escamoles Fried in Butter

INGREDIENTS

- 100 grams of escamoles
- Epazote (goosefoot, skunkweed, wormseed, or Mexican tea)
- Chopped onion
- Chopped garlic
- Serrano or jalapeño chilies
- Butter
- Salt, to taste
- Tortillas

DIRECTIONS

Thoroughly wash the escamoles and drain them. In a pan, add the butter. When it's melted, add the onion, garlic, and chilies, and sauté. Add the escamoles, the washed epazote, and the salt. Cook for a few minutes. Serve in tacos.

Ahuautles

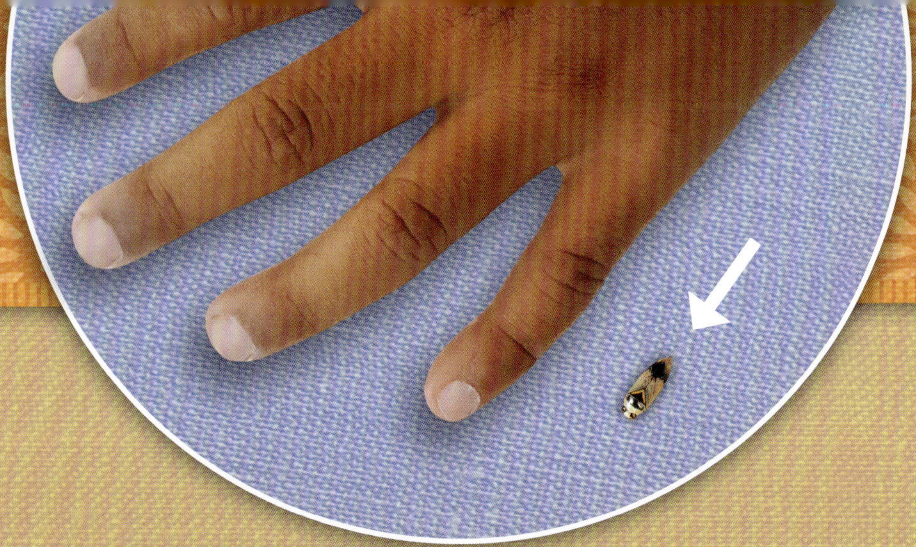

When?

They are collected during the months after the rainy season, usually between October and November.

What color are they?

They are sand color.

Ahuautles are the eggs of a type of water bug called axayácatl. It has big eyes, six legs, and is about the size of a small fingernail. It lives in lakes and uses two of its legs, in the form of oars, to swim. Even though it has two big wings, it rarely uses them. Why? It spends almost all of its life in the water.

A long time ago, many people ate these bugs. But nowadays, most are sold as bird, fish, and turtle food. What people now enjoy most is eating their eggs, which are laid by the thousands in the water and nearby plants. In Nahuatl, ahuautle means "water amaranth." They are so small that they resemble a little pile of sand. Once they are gathered and dried, they are ready to be prepared.

FUN FACT

Males try to attract females by making a chirping noise produced by rubbing their legs against their heads.

- Depending on the species, aquatic bugs live in lakes, lagoons, brooks, ponds, and other freshwater and saltwater bodies in different parts of the world.
- They measure from 3 to 20 millimeters and have six legs. The two front legs are used to grasp food and to hold on to aquatic plants. The two back legs, long and covered in tiny hairs, help them swim fast.
- The eggs, which cling to the underwater parts of plants, take from seven to fifteen days to incubate. In Mexico, they are harvested mainly in Lake Texcoco, in the State of Mexico. The adults are toasted before they are eaten, and the eggs are considered the Mexican caviar.
- Even though the adults spend most of the time in the water, they fly at night to look for a partner, to lay eggs in the plants near the shore, and to search for another place to live.
- It was reported by chroniclers that, when the Spanish conquerors first arrived in what would later be known as Mexico, Emperor Moctezuma enjoyed the insects and the eggs so much that, every morning during the season, runners brought them fresh from Lake Texcoco to Tenochtitlán for his breakfast.

Eggs with Ahuautles

INGREDIENTS

- 5 or 6 eggs
- Chopped onion
- 2 or 3 serrano or jalapeño chilies, chopped
- 1 1/2 tablespoons of ahuautles per egg
- Salt, to taste
- Vegetable oil

DIRECTIONS

Scramble the eggs, then add the onions, chilies, and ahuautles, and mix well. Heat the oil in a pan and add the mixture. Let it cook on one side, then flip to the other side to finish cooking. Or if you prefer, simply make them scrambled.

Cigarras

When cigarras, or cicadas, are larvae, they live underground and feed on the roots of trees. Once they emerge from the ground, they grow, sing very loudly, reproduce, and die within a few weeks. Because of the peculiar noise it makes, in Mexico a cigarra is also known as a chicharra—something that makes a buzzing sound.

Cigarras can be found on the tops of trees. People who like to eat them bring them down with a very long stick that has a piece of chewed gum on the end. Careful aim is required to tap the cigarra so it sticks to the gum.

When?

They are collected during the hot season, between May and June.

What color are they?

They are green.

FUN FACT

Adult cigarras live for less than a month, but when they are larvae, some can spend up to 17 years below the ground!

- It is thought that there are about 3,000 types of cicadas around the world.
- The mouths of larvae can transform into a type of bill, which is used to suction the sap of plants.
- Aristotle, the famous philosopher, said that the most delicious cicadas were the nymphs.
- Females lay their eggs in the ground or in tree bark and die soon thereafter.
- The larvae are diggers and will feed on plant roots.

Stewed Cigarras

INGREDIENTS

- Cigarras
- Caldillo (tomato broth), prepared to taste with one or two avocado leaves
- Salt, to taste
- Optional: Chopped chilies can be added to the tomato broth.

DIRECTIONS

Wash the cigarras very well. Carefully remove the head, including the insides. It's also convenient to remove the wings and the last segment of the legs. Then they can be toasted or fried and added to the previously prepared tomato broth.

Gusanos eloteros

When?

The worms are abundant during corn season, from May to September.

What color are they?

Their color can vary from light green to dark brown. Some also have black spots.

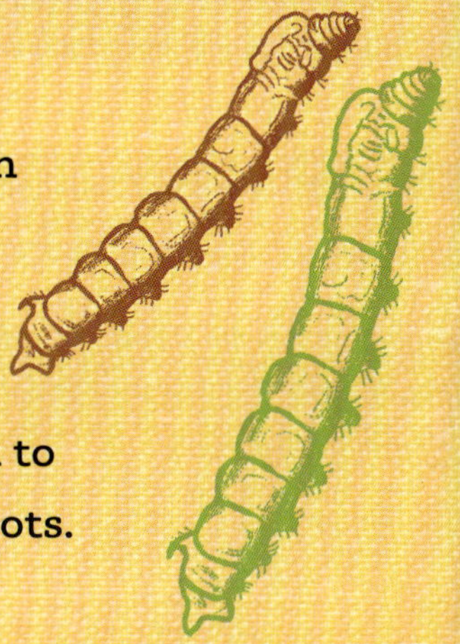

After a nocturnal moth lays her eggs on the topmost point of an ear of corn, the larvae are born in the shape of a worm. The spines found all over the bodies of these corn worms are so tiny that they can only be seen with a magnifying glass.

They feed on the corn. First, they eat the corn silk. Then, the kernels. This is why they taste like corn. When kids are in the cornfields, they open the ears of corn to look for worms. If they're lucky and find them, they will put them into a gourd or a bag to take home to be cooked.

FUN FACT

Even though the moth lays more than one egg in each ear of corn, generally only one worm survives—because they eat one another.

- Besides feeding on corn, it also eats tomatoes, cotton, green beans, lettuce, and soybeans, and can cause serious damage to crops.

- Once the elotero larva develops and becomes a pupa, it usually falls to the ground and burrows under. It will spend the winter there and, turned into an adult, it will emerge as a moth.
- The moth has green eyes, and its wings are beige with dark spots.
- Each egg, either white or yellowish, is half the size of the head of a pin.
- The worm can grow to 5 centimeters long.

Toasted Worms

INGREDIENTS

- Corn worms
- Salt, to taste
- Tortillas
- Your favorite salsa

DIRECTIONS

Wash the worms well and dry them. Toast them on a hot comal and sprinkle them with salt. Once they blow up and are crispy, they'll be ready to eat in a taco with salsa.

Libélulas

Libélulas, or dragonflies, are some of the most ancient insects in the world. A fossilized ancestor, from about 300 million years ago, had a wingspan ranging from 65 to 70 centimeters. Today, the wingspan of dragonflies ranges from just 5 to 12 centimeters.

When?

All year.

What color are they?

The adults are of many bright colors. When they fly, their iridescent wings reflect the light of the sun.

FUN FACT

The dragonfly is the insect that flies the best because it can fly in reverse, hover, and reach speeds of 48 kilometers per hour.

They have six legs with sharp barbs that allow them to perch on plants. They glide, swoop, and soar near lakes, swamps, and rivers. They lay their eggs near the shores or in the water. The nymphs—young dragonflies without wings—are what are eaten as an appetizer.

- Dragonflies have a pair of very close and large compound eyes. Each eye has about 30,000 facets. This allows them to have excellent 360-degree vision. With those eyes a dragonfly can spot its food even behind its head.

- Nymphs between 2 and 5 years of age live underwater. They breathe through gills and are carnivorous, devouring everything that comes their way, including other insects and fish.

- While in nymph stage, they can shed their skin between nine and seventeen times before becoming adults.

- In Mexico, you can buy nymphs in some markets of Hidalgo, the State of Mexico, and Quintana Roo. In Mexico City, you can find them in Xochimilco and Milpa Alta.

- The smallest dragonfly has wings that measure, wing tip to wing tip, 2 centimeters.

Scrambled Eggs with Dragonfly Nymphs

INGREDIENTS

- 4 eggs
- Salt and pepper, to taste
- 150 grams of dragonfly nymphs
- Vegetable oil or butter

DIRECTIONS

Scramble the eggs with salt and pepper, to taste. Add the nymphs, previously washed, drained, and dried. In a pan, heat the oil or butter and add the mixture. As the eggs start to set, gently pull them across the pan with a spatula or spoon, until they're cooked to taste. Bet you can't eat only one bite!

AUTHOR

Judy Goldman was born in Mexico City and still lives there today. She is the author of more than 50 books for kids published in Mexico, the United States, Brazil, and Colombia. She loves tacos, enchiladas, anything that has cinnamon in it, and the smell of freshly cut grass.

PHOTOGRAPHER

Ilán Rabchinskey is a Mexican artist and photographer who has traveled far and wide taking pictures for many books and magazines. Ever since he was little, he has enjoyed observing insects that live in gardens, especially the fireflies that come with the rainy season and light up the night. He has eaten many of the bugs that are described in this book. His favorites are the jumiles. He lives with Tsina, his Mexican hairless dog, in a century-old building in the center of Mexico City.